D1527223

RUTHLESS DESIRE

A Billionaire Dark Romance

By T. Bose

TABLE OF CONTENTS

CHAPTER ONE:
THE DEBT I NEVER OWED

I always thought the worst thing my father could do was gamble away our money.

I was wrong.

The moment I stepped into the dimly lit lounge of *La Fortuna*, I knew something was terribly wrong. The air was thick with smoke, the scent of expensive cologne mingling with the tension of men who had more power than they deserved. My pulse drummed in my ears as I scanned the room, searching for my father.

I found him slumped over a leather chair, his hands trembling as he clutched a glass of whiskey.

"You came," he rasped, looking up at me with bloodshot eyes.

My stomach knotted. "What the hell is going on, Dad?"

Before he could answer, a voice cut through the air like a blade.

"She's here."

I turned sharply. And that was the first time I saw him.

Cassian Morelli.

He sat with a glass of bourbon in hand, his gaze as sharp as a predator's. The dim light caught the angles of his face—strong jaw, piercing gray eyes, lips that looked like they never smiled. Dressed in a tailored black suit, he exuded power, danger, and something else I couldn't place.

My father's entire body tensed. He was afraid. **Afraid of him.**

Cassian leaned forward, resting his forearms on the table. "Your father has made a mess of things, Isla."

I swallowed hard. "What do you mean?"

Cassian took a slow sip of his drink before setting it down. "He owes me three million dollars."

The room spun. "Three—what?"

"Million," he confirmed. "And since he's proven himself incapable of paying, I've taken another form of payment."

His eyes dragged over me in a way that sent a shiver down my spine. Not lustful, not kind. **Possessive.**

"No." My voice came out hoarse. "No, that's not—"

"It's already done."

I turned to my father, desperate for him to deny it. But he wouldn't meet my eyes.

My knees threatened to give out.

Cassian stood, the movement slow, calculated. He was taller than I expected, towering over me with a presence that stole the air from my lungs. When he reached me, he lifted my chin with two fingers, forcing me to look at him.

"I own you now, Isla." His voice was low, smooth like silk wrapped around steel. "And there's nothing you can do about it."

CHAPTER TWO:
A CAGE OF GOLD AND CHAINS

I should have run.

I should have screamed, fought, done something.

But when you stare into the eyes of a man like Cassian Morelli, you realize something terrifying—*there is no escape.*

The silence in the room pressed against my skull, suffocating me. My father wouldn't even look at me, his shoulders slumped in quiet defeat.

"Let's go," Cassian ordered, his grip firm around my wrist.

I yanked my arm back. "I'm not going anywhere with you."

He raised an eyebrow, as if amused. "You think you have a choice?"

His words were like ice down my spine. "I'm not some object to be traded."

His lips curled into something that wasn't quite a smile. "You are now."

The humiliation burned through me, but before I could lash out, two men in suits stepped forward. Cassian didn't even have to gesture; his presence alone commanded them.

I was trapped.

I turned to my father one last time. "Please, tell me this isn't real. Tell me you didn't—"

His silence was my answer.

My heart cracked, something breaking inside me.

Cassian sighed, as if I was a mild inconvenience rather than a woman whose life he had just stolen. "Enough."

His fingers wrapped around my wrist again, firmer this time. I tried to fight him off, but his grip was like iron. He pulled me toward the door, past the guards, past the smoke and the whispers of men who had watched my fate be sealed like some twisted transaction.

Once we stepped outside, the night air hit me like a slap. A sleek black car was parked at the curb, its engine purring low like a beast waiting to strike.

I dug my heels into the ground. "I'm not going with you."

Cassian sighed again, his patience clearly wearing thin. "You will."

"And if I don't?" I spat.

He leaned in, so close I could feel the warmth of his breath against my skin. His scent—expensive, dark, laced with danger—invaded my senses.

"Then I make sure your father regrets every last mistake he's made."

A cold, ruthless promise.

I sucked in a shaky breath. "You're a monster."

He didn't flinch. "And you're mine now."

Tears burned behind my eyes, but I refused to let them fall. I refused to let him see me break.

With a resigned exhale, I let him lead me to the car.

The door clicked shut behind me, sealing me in.

And as the car pulled away, I realized something chilling.

This wasn't just captivity.

This was **possession**.

CHAPTER THREE:
A DEAL WITH THE DEVIL

The silence inside the car was thick, suffocating. The city lights blurred past the tinted windows, but I barely noticed. My hands curled into fists against my lap, my pulse hammering so hard I thought my ribs might crack under the weight of it.

Cassian sat beside me, a dark presence that took up too much space. He didn't speak. He didn't even look at me. He just sat there, completely at ease, while my entire world crumbled.

I turned toward him, my voice barely steady. "Where are you taking me?"

His fingers tapped against the leather seat, slow and deliberate. "Home."

The word sent a chill through me. "I have a home."

He finally looked at me then, his gray eyes unreadable. "Not anymore."

A lump formed in my throat, but I forced myself to lift my chin. "You can't just—just take me like this. This isn't legal. This isn't—"

His chuckle was low and dark. "Sweetheart, legality has nothing to do with power. And I have all the power."

I swallowed hard. "You don't own me."

He tilted his head slightly, regarding me like I was something fragile, something amusing. Then he leaned in, his voice a whisper against my skin.

"I do."

I jerked away, my pulse slamming against my veins. "You're insane."

He smirked but didn't deny it.

The car slowed as we approached a towering glass building, its presence dominating the skyline. My stomach twisted. I knew this place. *Morelli Tower.* The penthouse at the top was where Cassian Morelli lived.

And now, apparently, *where I would be kept.*

The driver opened my door, but I didn't move. I sat frozen, as if staying in the car would somehow change my fate.

Cassian sighed. "If you make me drag you out, I promise you won't like the consequences."

I turned to him sharply. "Is that supposed to scare me?"

His gaze was unreadable as he said, "No, Isla. It's supposed to warn you."

A shiver ran down my spine, but I forced my legs to move. The second my feet hit the ground, I considered running. But before I could even take a breath, Cassian's hand pressed against the small of my back, guiding me forward.

The touch was light, barely there. But the message was clear.

There was **no escaping him**.

The elevator ride was silent. My pulse pounded against my ribs as I watched the numbers climb higher and higher. Each second felt like a countdown to something I couldn't predict.

Then, the doors slid open.

His penthouse was... breathtaking. Floor-to-ceiling windows showcased the glittering city below, sleek modern furniture filling the vast space. But it wasn't the luxury that made my stomach knot.

It was the fact that I was **trapped** here.

Cassian walked inside like he owned the world. Maybe he did.

I stayed near the elevator, my arms crossed tightly over my chest. "What now? You expect me to be your obedient little pet?"

He turned slowly, his expression unreadable. "I expect you to be smart."

I scoffed. "And if I'm not?"

His smile was cold. "Then we'll have a problem."

My heart slammed against my ribs.

He took slow steps toward me, his presence a storm rolling in. "You don't have to like me, Isla. But you will respect me."

I clenched my fists. "You want respect? Try not **kidnapping** women."

His jaw ticked. "I didn't kidnap you. I claimed what was owed to me."

I glared at him, hating the calm arrogance in his voice. "I am not a *thing* to be claimed."

His eyes darkened. "Aren't you?"

8

I sucked in a breath as he reached out, brushing a loose strand of hair from my face. The touch was light, careful even, but it burned through me like fire.

I hated how my body reacted to him. Hated how the air between us crackled with something I couldn't name.

"You're playing a dangerous game, Isla," he murmured. "And I don't lose."

I jerked away, my heart thundering. "I will never belong to you."

He smirked. "We'll see."

And somehow, I knew he meant it.

CHAPTER FOUR:
A BEAUTIFUL CAGE

The door clicked shut behind me, sealing me in.

I stood frozen in the middle of Cassian Morelli's penthouse, my pulse drumming a frantic rhythm in my ears. The city lights glittered outside the towering windows, casting long shadows against the sleek marble floors. Everything about this place screamed **luxury**, but to me, it felt like a prison.

Cassian watched me with the patience of a predator, his hands tucked into his pockets, his expression unreadable.

"You should get some rest," he finally said.

I let out a sharp, humorless laugh. "You seriously expect me to just—what? Settle in? Pretend like this is normal?"

His eyes darkened slightly, but his voice remained calm. "I expect you to accept reality, Isla. The sooner you do, the easier this will be."

I took a step back, my arms crossing tightly over my chest. "And what exactly is *this*, Cassian? Am I your prisoner? Your...property?" I spat the last word, the taste of it bitter on my tongue.

A slow smirk curved his lips. "You're mine."

The way he said it sent an unwilling shiver through me. His voice was low, firm, **absolute**—as if the world itself had bent to his will.

I lifted my chin. "I'll never be yours."

His smirk faded, and for a brief second, something flickered in his eyes—something **dangerous**. He took a step toward me, and instinctively, I took a step back.

"Tell me, Isla," he murmured, "are you afraid of me?"

I swallowed hard, refusing to show weakness. "No."

He exhaled a quiet laugh, as if amused by my lie. "You should be."

My heart slammed against my ribs as he reached into his pocket and pulled out a sleek black keycard. He handed it to me, his fingers grazing mine for the briefest second.

"This is for your room."

I blinked, thrown off by the sudden gesture. "My...room?"

He nodded toward a hallway at the far end of the penthouse. "You'll stay here. You'll have your own space, your own freedom—within reason." His voice lowered. "As long as you don't try to run."

I hesitated. "And if I do?"

His jaw tensed. "You won't like the consequences."

The warning sent a chill down my spine, but I refused to let it show. Instead, I grabbed the keycard and stalked toward the hallway, my every step fueled by silent defiance.

I found the room easily. When I stepped inside, I nearly gasped.

It was **beautiful**.

A massive bed, draped in deep charcoal sheets, stood against one wall. A vanity, a walk-in closet, even a balcony overlooking the city—it was the kind of luxury most people would kill for.

But all I saw was a **gilded cage**.

I turned just as Cassian appeared in the doorway. He leaned against the frame, watching me with that infuriating calm.

"Get some sleep, Isla."

I lifted my chin. "Go to hell."

His lips twitched, as if I amused him. "Sweet dreams."

Then he was gone, the door clicking shut behind him.

I stood there for a long moment, my breathing uneven, my thoughts racing.

I was trapped. But I wouldn't break.

Not for Cassian Morelli.

Not for anyone.

CHAPTER FIVE:
THE CHAINS YOU CAN'T SEE

Sleep never came.

I lay in the massive bed, staring at the ceiling, listening to the faint hum of the city outside. No matter how soft the sheets were or how expensive the mattress felt beneath me, this wasn't comfort. It was **control**.

Cassian Morelli thought he owned me.

He thought power and money gave him the right to take what he wanted.

But he was wrong.

Morning light seeped through the balcony doors, painting golden streaks across the floor. I sat up slowly, exhaustion heavy in my bones. My body was still here, in this beautiful prison, but my mind was already forming plans.

I **would** find a way out.

A quiet knock at the door made me tense.

I didn't answer, but the door opened anyway.

Cassian.

He stood there in dark slacks and a crisp white dress shirt, the top two buttons undone. He looked effortless, powerful, like a man who controlled everything around him—including me.

"Did you sleep?" His voice was low, unreadable.

I swallowed down my exhaustion. "Like a baby."

His lips curved slightly, but I didn't miss the sharpness in his eyes. He knew I was lying.

"Get dressed," he said smoothly. "We have breakfast downstairs."

I scoffed. "Do I look like I have an appetite?"

He took a slow step forward. "I wasn't asking, Isla."

A surge of irritation flared through me, hot and unrelenting. "And if I say no?"

His gaze darkened. "Then I carry you."

The air between us **crackled**, thick with something neither of us would name. I hated how my pulse betrayed me, how my body tensed with awareness of just how **lethal** he was.

"You're insane," I muttered.

Cassian smirked. "And you're stubborn."

I folded my arms. "Fine. But only because I don't want to be manhandled first thing in the morning."

His eyes gleamed with something wicked, something **dangerous**. "Good girl."

The words sent a heat through me I didn't want to acknowledge.

I grabbed clothes from the closet—because of course it was stocked in my size—and disappeared into the en-suite bathroom before he could say another word.

Breakfast was waiting when I stepped into the dining area. A long glass table stretched across the room, set with fresh fruit, pastries, and steaming coffee.

Cassian sat at the head of the table, sipping his drink like he owned the world.

Which, in some ways, he did.

I hesitated at the threshold, my instincts screaming at me to keep my distance. But I wouldn't let him intimidate me.

I sat down, keeping as much space between us as possible.

Cassian watched me with quiet amusement. "You don't trust me."

I let out a dry laugh. "What was your first clue?"

He tilted his head. "Most women would kill to be in your position."

I arched an eyebrow. "Then give them my spot."

His smirk didn't waver. "I don't want them."

A chill ran through me. His words were simple, but the weight behind them was suffocating. **He wanted me.**

And that terrified me.

I focused on my coffee, ignoring the way his eyes never left me.

"You're trying to figure out how to escape," he mused.

I froze for half a second before forcing myself to take another sip. "I don't know what you're talking about."

Cassian leaned forward, resting his forearms on the table. "You won't get far, Isla. If you run, I will find you."

My breath caught, but I refused to look at him.

He continued, his voice softer now, more lethal. "And if I have to chase you, you won't like what happens when I catch you."

Something inside me twisted, equal parts fear and something darker—something I didn't dare name.

I forced a smirk, even as my heart pounded. "You like control, don't you?"

Cassian exhaled a quiet laugh. "I don't like it, Isla." His voice dropped to a whisper. "I **own** it."

His words wrapped around me like a velvet cage, and for the first time since this nightmare began, I realized something terrifying.

Cassian Morelli wasn't just dangerous.

He was **obsessed**.

And I didn't know if I would survive it.

CHAPTER SIX:
ESCAPE IS A DANGEROUS GAME

I waited until Cassian left.

The moment the front door shut behind him, I sprang into action.

I didn't know where he was going, and I didn't care. He had left me alone in this **gilded prison**, and that was his first mistake.

I moved quickly, checking every possible exit.

The front door? Locked with a biometric scanner.

The windows? Too high up—unless I suddenly grew wings, I wasn't getting out that way.

But the balcony…

I stepped outside, gripping the railing. A dizzying drop stretched below me, but to the right, a narrow ledge ran along the building's exterior. It wasn't **safe**, but neither was staying here.

If I could just get to the emergency stairwell—

The sound of footsteps behind me made my stomach drop.

My body locked up. I turned slowly, pulse hammering.

Cassian.

He stood in the doorway, arms folded, **completely unreadable**. The wind ruffled his dark hair, but his expression remained cold.

My heart thundered. "You left."

His lips quirked. "Did you think I wouldn't come back?"

I swallowed hard. "I was just getting fresh air."

Cassian took a slow step forward, and suddenly, the balcony felt **too small**.

"Were you?" His voice was smooth, controlled.

I forced my chin up. "I'm not your prisoner."

His eyes darkened. "No, you're not. But you're **mine**."

I inhaled sharply as he closed the distance, his presence swallowing the air around me. His fingers brushed my wrist, just a whisper of a touch, but it sent heat curling down my spine.

Cassian leaned in, his voice a low warning. "You have two choices, Isla."

My breath hitched. "And what are those?"

His hand slid to my waist, firm but not rough. A silent reminder of his **control**.

"You can walk inside on your own." His voice was velvet and steel. "Or I carry you."

I clenched my teeth. "You wouldn't—"

He smirked. "Try me."

For a long moment, neither of us moved. The tension stretched so tight it was suffocating.

Then, with a frustrated exhale, I turned and walked inside.

Cassian followed, shutting the balcony doors behind him.

I spun to face him. "You can't keep me here forever."

He studied me for a long second. Then he murmured, **"You think this is about keeping you?"**

My stomach twisted. There was something in his voice—something **dark**, something **obsessive**—that sent a shiver down my spine.

Before I could respond, his phone buzzed.

His expression hardened as he checked the screen.

A shadow passed over his face, and when he looked at me again, something had shifted.

"We're going out."

I frowned. "What?"

Cassian tucked his phone away. "Get dressed. Now."

A warning bell went off in my head. **Something was wrong.**

I didn't ask questions. I just grabbed my coat and followed him out the door.

The moment we stepped into the car, I felt it.

Danger.

Cassian was tense, his jaw locked, his eyes scanning the city streets as we drove. The easy arrogance was gone, replaced with something sharper, something lethal.

I hesitated. "Cassian...what's going on?"

He didn't answer immediately. Then, finally, he said, "Someone has been watching you."

A chill ran down my spine. "What?"

His grip on the steering wheel tightened. "I have enemies, Isla. And they know about you."

I sucked in a breath. "So what, I'm…bait?"

Cassian's head snapped toward me, his eyes flashing. "You are **not** bait."

I exhaled shakily. "Then what am I?"

His voice dropped. "Mine to protect."

His words shouldn't have sent a shiver through me. They shouldn't have made my pulse flutter with something I refused to name.

But they did.

I stared at him, my heart pounding. "Where are we going?"

Cassian's lips pressed into a thin line. "Somewhere safe."

I looked out the window, the city blurring past. I didn't know where we were going, or what we were walking into.

But one thing was clear.

Cassian Morelli wasn't just a billionaire with control issues.

He was a man with **enemies**.

And now, I was caught in the crossfire.

CHAPTER SEVEN:
THE WOLVES ARE WATCHING

The drive was silent.

Cassian's grip on the steering wheel was tight, his jaw locked, his entire body humming with tension. I'd never seen him like this before.

Cold. Calculating. **Deadly.**

Something was **wrong**.

I turned toward him, my pulse hammering. "Cassian, tell me the truth. Who's watching me?"

His eyes stayed fixed on the road. "A man named Viktor Mikhailov."

A shiver ran down my spine. I didn't know the name, but the way Cassian said it—like it was a curse, like it was **personal**—made my stomach knot.

"Why would he be watching me?" I demanded.

Cassian didn't answer right away. When he finally spoke, his voice was **controlled**, but there was something dark beneath it.

"Because he wants to hurt me."

I inhaled sharply. "So he's using me to get to you?"

Cassian's fingers flexed against the leather. "He's trying."

I swallowed hard. "And what does he want?"

His gaze flicked toward me, cold and unreadable. "To take what belongs to me."

My breath caught.

The **way** he said it—his voice deep, possessive, **unchallenged**—sent a heat curling through me. I hated that my body reacted, that my heart pounded **not just from fear but something else**.

I shook my head, shoving the thought away. "I don't belong to you."

Cassian exhaled a quiet laugh, but there was no humor in it. "Viktor thinks otherwise."

My stomach twisted. "And what happens if he gets to me first?"

His expression turned **ruthless**. "He won't."

A dark promise.

A vow made in **blood and vengeance**.

Cassian pulled the car into an underground garage, his movements precise and calculated. The moment the engine shut off, he turned to me.

"You don't leave my side."

A shiver ran down my spine. "Why do I feel like you're not telling me everything?"

His lips pressed into a thin line. "Because I'm not."

I stared at him, my heart hammering. "Cassian—"

"Get out."

His tone brooked no argument.

I swallowed hard and pushed the door open. The second my feet hit the ground, Cassian was at my side, his hand pressing against the small of my back as he guided me toward a sleek elevator.

We stepped inside, the tension between us thick enough to choke on.

As the doors slid shut, I exhaled. "So where are we?"

Cassian's eyes didn't leave the panel as he pressed the top floor. "Safehouse."

I frowned. "You have a *safehouse*?"

His smirk was faint, humorless. "I have **several**."

The idea that Cassian Morelli needed safehouses—that he had *enemies dangerous enough to warrant them*—sent a cold chill through me.

The doors slid open to reveal a **stunning penthouse**, but unlike his other one, this place felt...different.

Darker.

More secluded.

My stomach knotted. "How long are we staying here?"

Cassian closed the door behind us, locking it with a code. Then he turned to face me, his expression unreadable.

"As long as it takes."

I swallowed. "For what?"

His gaze darkened.

"For Viktor to make his move."

I exhaled sharply, fear curling through me. "You're using me as bait."

Cassian took slow, measured steps toward me. **A predator closing in.**

"No, Isla," he murmured. "I'm keeping you close. Because if Viktor touches you—if he even tries—" His voice dropped to something lethal. "I will burn his entire world to the ground."

My breath caught.

This man was dangerous. Unhinged. **Obsessed.**

And for the first time, I wasn't sure who I should be more afraid of—Cassian Morelli or the men coming for me.

CHAPTER EIGHT:
THE PREDATOR STRIKES

The air inside the safehouse was thick with tension.

Cassian stood by the window, watching the street below with a deadly stillness. The only sound was the faint hum of the city outside, but even that felt **too quiet**.

Something was coming.

I could feel it.

I hugged my arms around myself. "So what now?"

Cassian turned slightly, his gaze locking onto mine. "Now, we wait."

I exhaled sharply. "For what? For Viktor to just waltz in here and—"

A sharp **buzz** cut through the air.

Cassian's phone.

He answered immediately, his voice clipped. "What?"

Silence.

Then his jaw tightened, his knuckles turning white against the phone.

"When?" His voice was low, lethal.

Another pause.

Then, **"We're ready."**

A cold shiver ran down my spine.

Cassian ended the call and turned to me, his expression unreadable. "Stay here."

I frowned. "What? No."

His eyes darkened. "Isla."

I stepped toward him, my heart hammering. "You can't just—"

The **lights flickered**.

My breath caught.

Cassian's body **went rigid**, every muscle coiled like a predator sensing an ambush. His hand slid into his jacket, and when he pulled it out, I saw the glint of **a gun**.

Fear slammed through me.

Cassian turned to me, his voice sharp. "Do exactly as I say."

The next second, **the windows shattered.**

A deafening crack split the air as **gunfire erupted**, glass exploding around us.

Cassian lunged, grabbing me and pulling me down behind the marble kitchen island as bullets ripped through the walls. My pulse **screamed**, terror choking the breath from my lungs.

They found us.

Cassian's grip was iron around me, his voice low in my ear. "Stay down."

I trembled, my mind racing. "Cassian—"

"Shh." His eyes flicked toward the shattered windows, calculating. Then, to me: **"Do you trust me?"**

My pulse **stalled**.

Did I?

This man **stole me. Owned me. Controlled me.**

But right now, in this moment—**he was all I had**.

I swallowed hard. "Yes."

Something **shifted** in his eyes. Then he reached into his jacket, pulled out another gun, and pressed it into my shaking hands.

"Then run when I tell you."

Before I could respond, Cassian rose **like a god of war**, his gun firing in rapid succession. The men outside **shouted**, their figures moving through the shattered glass.

Viktor's men.

I **clutched the gun**, my breathing ragged. Then Cassian turned to me, his voice a **command**.

"Go."

CHAPTER NINE:
STOLEN BY THE ENEMY

Cassian's command **echoed** in my ears.

"Go."

I scrambled to my feet, my pulse hammering, the gun Cassian gave me clutched tightly in my shaking hands. The safehouse was filled with smoke, dust, and the **sharp scent of gunfire.**

Cassian moved like a storm, his gun firing with precision, cutting down the intruders one by one. **A machine built for war.**

I sprinted toward the hallway, my mind screaming for me to move faster. **Get out. Escape.**

But the second I reached the exit—

A rough hand **snatched** me from behind.

I gasped, my body yanked back into the shadows. An **iron grip** wrapped around my waist, crushing the air from my lungs.

Then—**a whisper against my ear, smooth and taunting.**

"Got you, little dove."

A sharp, icy fear sliced through me. **Viktor.**

Before I could scream, something **cold and metallic** pressed against my temple.

A gun.

My breath hitched. My entire body locked up in **paralyzed terror.**

"Cassian," I choked out.

Viktor chuckled darkly. "Oh, he'll come for you. But it'll be too late."

I struggled, kicking out, **fighting like hell**, but his grip was like a vise.

Then—**darkness.**

A cloth pressed against my mouth, the sharp scent of chloroform flooding my senses. My vision **blurred**, my muscles going weak.

I barely registered the sound of Cassian **roaring my name** before the world went **black.**

Unknown Location

My head **throbbed**.

The first thing I noticed was **cold metal** biting into my wrists. I tried to move, but my hands were **bound above me**, chained to something unyielding.

Panic **spiked** through my veins.

The second thing I noticed? **I wasn't alone.**

A low chuckle filled the dimly lit space.

"Well, well, sleeping beauty finally wakes up."

I snapped my eyes open.

Viktor.

He lounged in a leather chair, his **cruel blue eyes** gleaming with amusement. His dark blond hair was slicked back, and he looked **too at ease**, like he hadn't just **kidnapped me at gunpoint**.

I tugged at my restraints. **"Let me go, you psychopath."**

He smirked. "You've got fire. No wonder Cassian likes you."

I glared. "Cassian will kill you."

Viktor exhaled a slow, mocking sigh. "Oh, I'm counting on it."

A chill ran down my spine. **This wasn't just about me. This was about Cassian.**

Viktor leaned forward, resting his elbows on his knees. "You're a smart girl, Isla. So tell me… how do you think this ends?"

I swallowed hard, my pulse **pounding**.

I knew exactly how it ended.

In **blood.**

In **fire.**

In **Cassian tearing the world apart to get me back.**

I just didn't know if I'd **survive it.**

CHAPTER TEN:
A WAR IN HIS NAME

I'd never known true fear until now.

The cold metal biting into my wrists. The dim, windowless room. The slow, calculated movements of **Viktor Mikhailov**, watching me like a man with **nothing to lose**.

I was bound. Helpless. **A pawn in a war between monsters.**

But if Viktor thought I'd **break easily**, he was dead wrong.

I kept my chin high, my voice sharp. "Do you always kidnap women, or is this just a special occasion?"

Viktor's lips curled into a smirk. "Only when they're valuable."

I swallowed down the panic rising in my throat. "I'm not valuable to you."

His expression darkened. "No. But you are to Cassian."

The air turned suffocating.

That's what this was about. Not me. **Cassian.**

Viktor leaned forward, his voice smooth as silk. "Tell me, Isla… how well do you know your lover?"

My stomach twisted. "He's not my—"

"Ah." Viktor clicked his tongue. "Don't lie, little dove. Cassian doesn't steal things he doesn't want."

I sucked in a breath, refusing to let him rattle me. "And what do you want, Viktor?"

He grinned, slow and cold. "To watch your precious billionaire burn."

A chill crept up my spine.

Viktor stood, circling me like a predator. "Cassian Morelli is a **man who takes**. A man who thinks the world is his playground." His voice sharpened. "But men like that always have **weaknesses**."

He stopped behind me, his breath warm against my ear. "And now, I have his."

My entire body locked up.

Viktor's fingers **brushed my shoulder**, deliberate, testing. I flinched before I could stop myself.

He laughed softly. "What do you think he'll do when he finds you like this?"

My stomach twisted.

He wanted to **provoke Cassian**. Wanted to **break him**.

I clenched my fists. "If you kill me, he'll rip you apart."

Viktor chuckled. "Who said anything about killing?"

My blood turned to ice.

The door suddenly burst open. A man in a suit stepped inside, his expression tense. "Sir. We have a problem."

Viktor's jaw ticked. "What kind of problem?"

The man hesitated. Then: **"Cassian Morelli just declared war."**

Cassian Morelli's Penthouse

Cassian sat at the head of the table, his gray eyes **lethal**, his fingers tapping against the polished wood.

The room was filled with his most dangerous men— bodyguards, enforcers, men who lived in the shadows.

And all of them were waiting for one thing.

His command.

Cassian exhaled slowly, controlled. Calculated.

Then, his voice dropped into something **lethal**.

"Find Viktor."

Silence.

Then one of his men—Luca, his second-in-command—nodded. "We already have a lead."

Cassian's grip **tightened**. "Then move."

Luca hesitated. "Boss… Viktor took her for a reason. He wants to break you. Wants you reckless."

Cassian's jaw ticked. "Then let him."

A muscle in Luca's cheek twitched. "And if it's a trap?"

Cassian leaned back, his smirk **cold**. "Then I'll set it on fire."

Luca nodded once, then left the room.

Cassian exhaled, running a hand over his jaw.

Then he reached for his **gun**.

Because Viktor had made a fatal mistake.

He took **what belonged to Cassian Morelli.**

And now?

Now, **he would burn.**

CHAPTER ELEVEN: FIRE AND BLOOD

Unknown Location – Viktor's Safehouse

The atmosphere in the room had changed.

Viktor was no longer **amused**.

He was **calculating**.

The second his man had whispered the words, *Cassian Morelli just declared war*, something **cold and ruthless** had settled in his sharp blue eyes.

I yanked at the restraints around my wrists, heart pounding. **Cassian was coming.**

I should have been relieved.

But Viktor was too calm. Too **prepared**.

He turned to me, tilting his head. "Your billionaire is predictable."

I clenched my jaw. "You're afraid of him."

His lips twitched. "No. I'm disappointed." He sighed, as if Cassian was a foolish child. "He always lets emotion get the better of him."

I glared. "You think this is about emotion?"

Viktor leaned in. "You tell me, little dove."

My pulse pounded as he dragged a knife from his belt, running the tip along my forearm. Not cutting— just **taunting**.

I didn't flinch. I wouldn't give him the satisfaction.

Viktor smirked. "Cassian will burn this city to find you. But what will he do when he realizes the truth?"

I swallowed. "What truth?"

His eyes gleamed. "That you were never just **collateral**."

A sick feeling settled in my stomach.

"What are you talking about?" I whispered.

Viktor straightened, slipping the knife back into his belt. "Oh, sweetheart." His smirk turned razor-sharp. "You really don't know, do you?"

I stared at him, every nerve in my body **screaming**.

What the hell was he talking about?

But before he could answer—

A deafening **BOOM** shook the building.

The lights **flickered**. The ground **rumbled**.

Then—a voice rang out over the chaos.

Cassian.

"VIKTOR!"

My entire body **froze**.

Because I'd never heard him like that before.

Rage. Possession. **Bloodlust.**

Cassian Morelli had come for me.

And he was ready to **burn the world down**.

Cassian's POV – Viktor's Safehouse

The second the **explosives** went off, Cassian moved.

His men were already inside, taking down Viktor's guards with **deadly precision**. But Cassian didn't care about them.

He only cared about **one thing**.

Isla.

His heart was a drum, pounding, violent, **feral**.

He stormed through the wreckage, gun in hand, **killing anything in his path**.

He wasn't thinking. **He was hunting.**

And when he finally reached the door at the end of the hall—

He didn't hesitate.

He **kicked it open**.

Viktor stood in the center of the room, a knife at Isla's throat.

Cassian's vision **blurred with rage**.

His **Isla**. Bound. **Terrified.**

His hand **tightened on the gun**, his voice cold.

"Let. Her. Go."

Viktor's smirk didn't waver. "Took you long enough."

Cassian didn't waste words.

He **fired**.

Viktor dodged, the bullet grazing his arm. But Cassian was already **moving**, crossing the room in seconds.

Viktor **lunged**. Cassian caught his wrist, twisting until the knife **clattered to the floor**. Then he drove his fist into Viktor's face, the sickening crack of bone ringing through the air.

Viktor staggered, blood dripping from his nose.

Cassian didn't stop.

Didn't hesitate.

He hit him **again. And again.**

Until Viktor was barely standing.

Until his knuckles were **slick with blood**.

Then, finally, Cassian grabbed him by the throat, slamming him against the wall. His voice was deadly quiet.

"You touched what's mine."

Viktor coughed, grinning through the blood. "Did I?"

Cassian's grip **tightened**. "Give me one reason not to put a bullet in your head."

Viktor's smile widened. "Because I know something you don't."

Cassian **froze**.

Viktor's swollen lips parted. "You really don't know, do you?" His voice was **mocking**, even as blood dripped down his face. "Poor Cassian. So powerful, yet so clueless."

Cassian's **pulse roared**. "Know what?"

Viktor chuckled darkly. "Why I took **her**."

Cassian's stomach **coiled**.

Then, Viktor whispered something so low Cassian almost didn't hear it.

38

And when he did—

Everything **stopped**.

The rage. The control. The air itself.

Because if Viktor was telling the truth—

Then Isla wasn't just a **pawn in a game.**

She was the **key to everything.**

CHAPTER TWELVE:
THE TRUTH IN BLOOD

Cassian's POV

Viktor's lips curled into a bloody grin, his voice hoarse but **mocking**.

"Tell me, Morelli... did you ever wonder why Isla was the one her father sold?"

Cassian's grip **tightened** around Viktor's throat, his pulse a thunderous roar in his ears. "Speak."

Viktor let out a strained chuckle. "You think this is a coincidence? That out of all the women in this city, her father just *happened* to owe *you*?"

Cassian's stomach **coiled**.

A sliver of doubt wormed its way into his rage.

No. He hadn't questioned it. He hadn't cared. Isla had been **given to him**, and he had **taken her**.

But now...

Now he wasn't so sure.

"What are you saying?" he demanded.

Viktor exhaled shakily, his smirk still in place despite the **blood coating his teeth**. "You don't know, do you?" He coughed, spitting red onto the floor. "She's not just some poor girl with a gambling father."

Cassian felt **Isla's gaze** on him now. He didn't turn, didn't dare look at her.

Because something **in his gut told him he wasn't going to like the answer.**

Viktor leaned in slightly, his voice **low, deadly.**

"She was meant to be yours all along."

The words landed like a gunshot.

Cassian's blood ran **cold**.

"No," Isla's voice **shook** behind him. "That's not possible."

Cassian finally turned, his chest **tight**, his heart pounding harder than it had during the fight.

Isla's face was pale, her hands still trembling where she had been tied. But her eyes—**wide, full of uncertainty**—were locked onto Viktor.

She was scared.

Because she wasn't sure he was **lying**.

Cassian turned back to Viktor. "Explain. Now."

Viktor smirked, his split lip curling. "Her father owed *me* first. But I let that debt slide. Why?" His blue eyes gleamed. "Because someone else wanted her."

Cassian's fingers **tensed** around Viktor's collar. "Who?"

Viktor's grin widened. "Your father."

The entire room **went still**.

Cassian's **chest constricted**. "What the hell are you talking about?"

Viktor let out a low laugh. "Oh, you don't know, do you?" His voice turned taunting, **mocking Cassian's ignorance**. "Daddy Morelli made a deal years ago.

Your inheritance was supposed to come with a *wife*. One chosen for you."

Cassian's **breath stalled**.

Isla **stiffened** behind him. "That's a lie."

Viktor's grin didn't falter. "Is it? Tell me, Isla—did your father ever mention *why* his debts always seemed to disappear? Did you ever wonder why, despite all the money he owed, he never ended up dead?"

Isla's lips parted, her **expression flickering with uncertainty**.

"No," she whispered. "No, my father never—" She cut off, her **brows furrowing**. A moment of hesitation.

Cassian saw it. And so did Viktor.

Viktor **chuckled darkly**. "That's right, little dove. He never told you. Because he knew that one day, when the time was right, you would belong to Cassian Morelli."

A muscle in Cassian's jaw **ticked**. "You're lying."

Viktor smirked. "Am I?"

Silence **stretched** between them, thick and suffocating.

Cassian's mind raced. He **knew** his father had controlled his future, arranged business mergers through marriages. But Isla?

Had his father really **planned this?**

Had he already **chosen her for him?**

A sickening realization **twisted in his gut**.

If Viktor was telling the truth…

Then Isla hadn't just been sold to Cassian by chance.

She had **always** been meant for him.

Fate, control, a game played by **dead men's hands**.

And neither of them had ever known.

Isla's POV

My heart **pounded violently**.

This couldn't be real.

It couldn't.

But a part of me—a small, treacherous part— **wondered**.

Why had my father **never let me leave the city**?

Why had his debts never led to **anything worse**?

And why, when he had finally lost everything, had I **been given to Cassian**—a man whose name carried power, but more importantly…

A man whose father had built an empire on blood and arranged marriages.

I sucked in a shaky breath. "Cassian…"

He didn't look at me.

His fists were **tight**, his muscles coiled like he was about to **explode**.

Viktor exhaled a slow, satisfied sigh. "You were both playing the wrong game." His gaze flicked to Cassian. "You didn't just steal her. You took what was already yours."

Cassian's breath was **ragged**, his **control slipping**.

I felt my own panic **rising**.

Because I wasn't just a **prisoner** anymore.

I was **his fate.**

And I didn't know if I could **survive that truth.**

Cassian's POV

He didn't **speak**.

Didn't **breathe**.

His father had planned this? **Had chosen her?**

And he had fallen right into the trap.

His grip tightened on Viktor's collar. He should have put a bullet in him by now. Should have ended this.

But his rage was tangled with **something deeper, something dangerous.**

Because Isla wasn't just **his** anymore.

She had always been.

Even before he'd known.

Even before she had fought him.

Even before **she had tried to escape him.**

And now?

Now, **there was no escape at all.**

CHAPTER THIRTEEN:
THE CHAINS OF FATE

Isla's POV

My world had just **shattered**.

I sat in the backseat of Cassian's car, my wrists still **raw from the restraints**, my body trembling—not from fear, not from exhaustion, but from the sick, **twisting truth** Viktor had just revealed.

I had never been free.

Not before Cassian. Not even before my father's debts.

Because from the moment I was **born**, my fate had been **sealed**.

My father had **never** planned to save me.

He had only been waiting for the right moment to hand me over to the **devil himself**.

I stared out the tinted window, my vision blurring with city lights. The world outside looked the same. But **I wasn't the same anymore**.

I felt **Cassian's gaze** on me, heavy and unreadable. He hadn't said a word since he dragged me from Viktor's grasp, since he killed anyone who had dared to stand between us.

I should have been **grateful**.

But how could I be?

How could I thank the man who had **saved me from one prison, only to claim me for his own?**

The car pulled into the underground parking of his penthouse, the engine cutting off with a deep purr.

Silence.

I forced a breath, gripping the door handle.

"Don't," Cassian said smoothly.

I froze.

His voice was **calm**, but there was something underneath it—**something sharp, unyielding.**

I turned slowly, meeting his eyes.

His **gray gaze burned into me**, his jaw locked tight, his entire body coiled like a predator on the verge of snapping.

"You're not running," he murmured.

A slow **warning**.

I lifted my chin. "I should."

His lips quirked, but there was **no humor in it**. "You won't get far."

Anger flared through me, battling the unease tightening in my ribs. "So, what now? You keep me locked up in your tower like a **possession?**"

Cassian exhaled a slow, measured breath. "You were always mine, Isla. Whether I knew it or not."

A shiver **rippled down my spine**.

The way he said it—**absolute, unchallenged, final**—made my stomach twist.

"I don't belong to you," I whispered.

Cassian's smirk was **dangerous**. "Then why does your pulse race every time I touch you?"

I sucked in a sharp breath as he **reached for me**, his fingers grazing my jaw. The heat of his skin **branded me**, sent something **dark and unrelenting curling through my veins**.

No.

I couldn't let him do this. Couldn't let him **twist fate into something I wanted**.

I shoved his hand away, my breath shaky. "This doesn't change anything."

Cassian's gaze darkened. "It changes **everything**."

Before I could move, his hand **shot out, gripping my wrist**.

Not hard. **Not to hurt.**

Just enough to tell me that **he would never let me go.**

My stomach **tightened**.

This wasn't love.

This was **obsession**.

Possession.

And the worst part?

I wasn't sure if I **hated it… or if I wanted it.**

Cassian's POV

She was **running in circles**.

I could see it in her eyes—the panic, the rage, the **undeniable attraction she refused to name**.

47

It was **adorable**.

And utterly **pointless**.

I let out a slow breath, watching as she yanked her wrist from my grip, her hands **shaking**, her body **betraying her own words**.

"You can fight it all you want," I said softly, stepping closer.

She **stiffened**, but she didn't move away.

She **never did**.

"But it won't change the truth," I murmured.

Her eyes snapped to mine, wide and **furious**. "And what truth is that, Cassian?"

I smirked, tilting my head.

"That you were always meant to be mine."

Her **breath hitched**.

Because she knew. **Deep down, she already knew.**

I leaned in slightly, my fingers grazing her hip. Her **pulse hammered against my touch**, her body betraying her **mind's stubborn fight**.

"You don't hate me," I murmured against her ear.

Her hands clenched into fists, her breathing ragged.

I dragged my fingers along the inside of her wrist, feeling the **wild thrum of her heartbeat.**

"Say it," I whispered.

Isla's lips parted, her eyes **stormy with something she refused to name**.

"I hate you," she whispered.

A slow smile spread across my lips.

"No, you don't."

Her breath **shuddered**.

Then, she shoved me **hard**, her pulse **wild**, her voice shaking with something close to **desperation**.

"You ruined my life."

I caught her wrist again, gently this time, my fingers **stroking her skin**.

"No, Isla." My voice dropped, low and **dangerous**.

"I gave you a new one."

She exhaled sharply, a sound caught between a gasp and a curse.

But she didn't run.

Not this time.

And that?

That was all the proof I needed.

Because **Isla Thornton already belonged to me.**

Now, it was only a matter of time before she **admitted it.**

CHAPTER FOURTEEN: RUN IF YOU DARE

Isla's POV

I couldn't breathe.

Not here.

Not in this **prison dressed as a penthouse**, where every inch of space was tainted by **him**.

Cassian Morelli.

My **captor. My fate. My downfall.**

I stared at him, heart pounding, my body still **humming** from his touch, from the way his fingers had traced my wrist like a silent **claim**.

I gave you a new life.

His words wrapped around me like a chain, heavy and unrelenting.

No.

No, I refused to let this be my life.

I wasn't his. **I wouldn't be his.**

I turned away, forcing my breath to steady. "I need to shower."

Cassian studied me, his sharp gray eyes **seeing too much**.

For a moment, I thought he'd refuse.

But then, he smirked. "Fine. But don't try anything, sweetheart."

I forced a small, tight smile. "Wouldn't dream of it."

Liar.

The second the bathroom door shut behind me, I **moved fast**.

Cassian had let me out of his sight—his **first mistake**.

My pulse thrummed as I ran the water, making it loud enough to mask my movements. Then I yanked open the window.

The **drop was brutal.**

Thirty stories up. No fire escape. No ledges wide enough to climb down.

But there was a **maintenance scaffold**, just a few feet out of reach.

I swallowed hard. **This is insane.**

But not as insane as **staying here**.

A breath. A silent prayer. Then—I jumped.

For one terrifying second, I was **falling**.

Then—**impact.**

I slammed against the metal frame, my fingers clawing desperately at the bars. Pain **flared** through my arms as I struggled to pull myself up.

My heart pounded wildly. **I did it.**

But then—

A low, **deadly** voice behind me.

"Going somewhere, little dove?"

No.

A violent **shudder** ripped through me as I twisted to see him.

Cassian stood at the window, one hand braced against the frame, his other holding his **gun** loosely at his side.

His expression? **Pure darkness.**

His jaw **ticked**, his gray eyes **burning with cold fury**.

For a long, excruciating second, neither of us moved.

Then—Cassian exhaled, **shaking his head slowly**.

"You just never learn, do you?"

A shiver rolled down my spine. **Run. Move. Do something.**

But my body refused to obey.

Cassian tilted his head, watching me like a **wolf who'd caught his prey but wasn't sure whether to kill it or play with it first**.

Then—he moved.

Fast. Lethal. Inescapable.

I barely had time to react before he **leaped out onto the scaffold**, landing in a smooth crouch.

A **hunter chasing what was already his.**

My pulse screamed. "Cassian, don't."

His smirk was **devastating**. "That's not how this works, Isla."

I turned, scrambling toward the ladder on the side of the scaffold. I didn't care where it led. Didn't care if I fell.

I just **needed to get away from him.**

But I'd barely made it three steps before **his hands grabbed me.**

A sharp gasp ripped from my throat as he yanked me **back against his chest**, his arms like steel bands around me.

I fought, kicking, struggling—**but it was useless.**

Cassian **never let go.**

"Enough," he growled against my ear, his breath **hot, furious.**

I thrashed, but his grip only **tightened**, pinning my arms to my sides.

"Let me go," I hissed.

His **laugh was dark.** "After that stunt?" He exhaled sharply, his grip **possessive, punishing.** "You just don't get it, do you?"

I froze as his lips brushed my ear.

"You were never going to escape me."

A violent shudder ran through me. "Cassian—"

He turned me in his arms, forcing me to **face him.**

His hands **caged my wrists** as he backed me against the railing, his gray eyes burning into mine.

"Tell me, Isla," he murmured. "Where exactly were you planning to go?"

I swallowed hard, my heart **slamming against my ribs.**

Anywhere but here.

But I couldn't say that.

Couldn't say anything.

Because the way he looked at me—the way his fingers **tightened around my skin, the way his voice wrapped around me like silk and steel**—made me feel like I'd already lost.

Like I'd **never stood a chance.**

His lips **ghosted over my cheek**, his breath **hot, unrelenting**.

"I gave you a chance," he whispered. "I warned you not to run."

I shuddered. "I can't stay here."

His fingers **tilted my chin up**, forcing me to look at him.

"Yes, you can."

Something snapped inside me.

Fury. Desperation. **Something else I refused to name.**

I shoved him **hard**, my voice cracking. "You can't just *keep* me, Cassian!"

His eyes darkened, his smirk slow and **deadly.**

"I already have."

I sucked in a sharp breath.

Because the worst part?

I didn't know if I still wanted to run.

CHAPTER FIFTEEN: PUNISHMENT AND SURRENDER

Isla's POV

I should have been terrified.

Cassian's grip on my wrists was **iron**, his chest rising and falling with deep, controlled breaths. His **gray eyes burned**with something dark, something sharp, something I didn't dare name.

And yet—**I wasn't afraid.**

I was **furious.**

"You can't just—" My voice **cracked**, but I forced myself to meet his gaze. "You can't keep doing this."

Cassian tilted his head, studying me like I was a puzzle he was **piecing together**. "Doing what?"

My pulse thundered. "Controlling me. Chasing me. Owning me."

His smirk was **slow**, devastating. "That's where you're wrong, sweetheart."

A shiver ran through me as he pressed closer, his fingers **trailing down my arm**, slow and deliberate.

"I don't just *own* you," he murmured. "I **am** you."

The words **hit like a drug**, intoxicating and lethal.

I shook my head, trying to force air into my lungs. "You—"

"You feel it, don't you?" His voice was **a quiet storm**, relentless. "The way you fight me, the way you run." His thumb **brushed my pulse point**, feeling the frantic beat beneath my skin. "But your heart always races for me."

My breath hitched. "That's not—"

His **grip tightened**, his body **looming over mine**, pinning me against the railing. "Lie to yourself all you want, Isla." His lips **hovered near mine**, so close it made my entire body **ache**. "But don't lie to me."

A **tremor** ran through me.

He was too close. Too **much**.

I needed to push him away. **Needed to fight.**

But when I opened my mouth, the words **wouldn't come**.

Because the truth was **devastating**.

The truth was—I didn't hate his touch.

I **craved it.**

And Cassian **knew it.**

His fingers traced the curve of my jaw, **gentle but firm**. "You ran from me," he murmured. "That deserves a punishment."

A slow **shiver** ran down my spine.

I **hated** how my body responded to those words.

Cassian watched me, his lips curving into something dark. **Something victorious.**

"You don't believe me?" he murmured.

Then, **he spun me around** in one swift motion, my back **colliding against his chest.**

I gasped. "Cassian—"

His hands **wrapped around my wrists**, pulling them behind me.

"You don't listen, Isla," he murmured against my ear, his breath **hot**, his touch **unforgiving**. "You never listen."

I **struggled**, but it was **pointless.**

His grip was **unshakable.**

His hold was **everything I feared... and everything I wanted.**

His lips **brushed my ear**, his voice a dangerous whisper.

"I told you what would happen if you ran."

A tremor ran through me. "You can't just—"

His hands **tightened**, pressing me **against him.**

My pulse **screamed.**

"I can. And I will."

I **hated** him.

I **wanted** him.

And worst of all?

I couldn't tell the difference anymore.

CHAPTER SIXTEEN: BOUND BY FIRE

Isla's POV

My breath came in ragged, shallow gasps.

Cassian's grip on my wrists was **unrelenting**, his body pressed **dangerously close**, his presence **all-consuming**.

I should have hated this.

I should have hated **him**.

But my body was a **traitor**, betraying me in the worst possible way.

I felt the heat of him against my back, the hard press of his fingers as they **tightened around my wrists**, pinning me in place. **Owning me.**

"You don't listen, Isla," he murmured, his breath brushing against my ear. **Taunting. Testing.**

I swallowed hard, my pulse hammering. "And what are you going to do about it?"

A slow, dangerous smirk. "Whatever I want."

A shiver ripped through me.

This was a game. A dangerous, unwinnable game. And Cassian Morelli?

He never lost.

I turned my head slightly, meeting his gaze. "You think you can break me?" My voice was breathless, but I forced steel into it.

Cassian exhaled a quiet laugh, low and **predatory**. "I don't need to break you, sweetheart." His fingers **trailed down my spine**, sending a bolt of **fire** through me. "You'll come to me willingly."

My stomach **coiled**. "Never."

His grip **tightened**, his eyes gleaming with something **ruthless**. "Then why do you tremble when I touch you?"

I sucked in a sharp breath.

Because he was **right**.

Because my body was betraying me in ways I didn't understand, in ways I **refused to accept**.

But I couldn't let him win.

I turned my face toward his, our lips almost **brushing**, my voice a whisper. "You think you own me?"

Cassian smirked. "I know I do."

I inhaled sharply. Then, with everything I had left, I **wrenched free**.

Cassian let me go—**no, he let me think I was free**—before catching me again, this time with **both hands wrapped around my waist, caging me in**.

His voice was low, dark, **final**.

"Run all you want, Isla." His fingers **dug into my skin**, a silent claim. "But you'll always end up back here."

I clenched my fists, my breathing uneven. "And what happens when I stop running?"

A slow, wicked smile.

"Then I keep you."

My heart **slammed** against my ribs.

Because the worst part?

I didn't know if I wanted to run anymore.

CHAPTER SEVENTEEN: THE LAST DEFIANCE

Isla's POV

His words hung in the air between us.

"Then I keep you."

A promise. A vow. **A sentence.**

I **hated** how my body responded to those words. The way my breath **hitched**, the way something dark and thrilling **curled in my stomach**.

Cassian saw it. He always **saw it**.

His grip on my waist was firm but **not unkind**. As if daring me to make a choice. As if he already knew how this would end.

And maybe he did.

Maybe he always had.

I swallowed hard. "And if I don't want to be kept?"

His smirk was slow, devastating. "Then why haven't you run yet?"

I sucked in a breath.

Because he was **right**.

I could have fought harder. I could have screamed. I could have clawed my way to the door, thrown myself into another escape attempt.

But I didn't.

I just stood there, **trapped in the heat of him**, unable to move, unable to do anything except **feel**.

His fingers trailed up my arm, **gentle, possessive**, leaving **fire in their wake**. "Say it, Isla."

I swallowed. "Say what?"

His smirk deepened. **"That you don't want me."**

My pulse **thundered**.

Say it. Say the words. **Break free.**

But when I opened my mouth—**nothing came out.**

Cassian's eyes gleamed. **Triumphant. Knowing.**

His hands **tightened on my waist**, pulling me **against him**, letting me feel every inch of the power he held over me.

"You can lie to yourself all you want," he murmured, his breath teasing my skin. "But you can't lie to me."

I let out a shaky breath. **He was winning.**

No—**he had already won.**

Cassian exhaled slowly, his fingers **brushing my jaw, tilting my chin up**. His voice was dark silk, **irrevocable and absolute**.

"You are mine, Isla."

My breath **shattered**.

Because I knew, in that moment, that there was only **one way this could end.**

And it wasn't with **me running.**

Cassian's POV

She wasn't fighting anymore.

Her pulse was **wild beneath my fingers**, her breaths **uneven**, her entire body betraying the war she was losing.

I had waited for this moment.

Waited for the **exact second she realized there was no escape.**

Not from me.

Not from **us**.

I leaned in, my lips grazing her ear. "Say it, sweetheart."

Her breath **hitched**.

I **felt** the surrender in her body.

The moment her walls **collapsed**, the moment she finally understood.

She was never meant to run.

She was meant to be **chased, caught, claimed.**

Isla let out a slow, shuddering exhale. Then—**she looked up at me.**

And whispered the words I had been waiting for.

"I was always yours."

A slow, wicked smile curled my lips.

Victory.

At last.

And now?

Now, I would never let her go.

CHAPTER EIGHTEEN: THE POINT OF NO RETURN

Isla's POV

The moment the words left my lips, I knew.

There was no taking them back.

No undoing what I had just done.

I was always yours.

Cassian's smirk was slow, **devastating**, his gray eyes gleaming with something dark and **triumphant**.

His grip on my waist **tightened**, his fingers pressing into my skin like a silent **claim**.

A slow breath.

A **moment suspended in time**.

Then—**he moved.**

One second, I was standing. The next, I was **pinned against the nearest wall**, my breath **snatched from my lungs**, my heart hammering against my ribs.

Cassian's hands **caged me in**, his body **looming over mine**, his presence **all-consuming**.

"You finally understand," he murmured.

I swallowed hard, my pulse **pounding in my throat**. "Cassian—"

He **shook his head**, his fingers tracing a slow, deliberate path down my arm. "No more fighting, Isla."

His voice was **a quiet command**, smooth and absolute.

A shudder rippled through me.

Because he was right.

I wasn't fighting anymore.

I couldn't.

Not when my body **melted into his**, not when my breath **hitched at his touch**, not when everything inside me **ached** for something I had spent too long denying.

Cassian saw it. **Felt it. Knew it.**

His smirk deepened. "Good girl."

A sharp, **dangerous thrill** shot through me.

I hated how easily those two words made my body tremble. How effortlessly he unraveled me.

How much I wanted him to **ruin me completely.**

My hands clenched at my sides. "I don't know how to do this," I whispered.

Cassian exhaled a quiet laugh, **low and sinful.** "You don't have to."

His fingers tilted my chin up, forcing me to meet his gaze.

"Just let me show you."

And I did.

Cassian's POV

She was mine now.

Finally. **Completely.**

And I would make sure she never forgot it.

I traced a slow line down her spine, savoring the way her breath **shuddered**, the way her body **yielded** despite the tension still lingering in her muscles.

"You don't have to be afraid, Isla," I murmured.

She inhaled sharply. "I'm not."

A slow smirk. "Liar."

She glared at me, but I could see it—the way her pulse **betrayed her**, the way her fingers **twitched**, as if unsure whether to push me away or **pull me closer**.

I leaned in, my lips brushing the shell of her ear.

"Say it again."

She **stilled**. "Say what?"

I let my teeth graze **lightly** over her pulse point, a warning, a **promise**.

"That you're mine."

Her breath caught.

For a moment, I thought she might fight me again.

But then—**she exhaled.**

Soft. Reluctant. **Inevitable.**

"I'm yours," she whispered.

A slow, **dark satisfaction** unfurled inside me.

Because now?

Now there was **no going back.**

For either of us.

CHAPTER NINETEEN:
THE COST OF BELONGING

Isla's POV

The moment I said the words, **I'm yours**, I felt the shift.

Something **unseen** cracked between us, something dark and irrevocable.

Cassian knew it.

I knew it.

And yet, as I sat curled in the plush chair in his penthouse, staring out at the glittering city lights, a knot of **doubt** twisted in my chest.

What had I done?

What did this **mean**?

I had spent weeks fighting him, trying to escape, convincing myself that this wasn't **real**. That he had only taken me because of a **deal, a transaction, a debt not my own**.

But now, something was different.

Something was **deeper**.

And it scared me.

Because when I looked at Cassian—when I **felt** his presence behind me, when I heard the way his voice softened **just slightly** when he said my name—I realized something dangerous.

I didn't just belong to him.

I wanted to.

The thought **terrified** me.

I exhaled shakily, pressing my fingers to my temples.

I needed air.

I needed **space.**

I pushed up from the chair and padded toward the door.

Cassian's voice stopped me instantly.

"Where are you going?"

I turned slowly. He stood near the fireplace, his jacket tossed over the couch, his sleeves rolled up. **Effortless power. Dangerous control.**

My throat tightened. "I just... need a moment."

Cassian's eyes darkened.

"A moment?" His voice was **silk and steel**, a quiet warning.

I nodded. "I just—"

"Let me be clear, Isla," he murmured, stepping closer. **Lethal. Certain.**

"You don't walk away from me."

My stomach **tightened**. "I just need to think."

His smirk was slow, **devastating**. "Think about what?"

I swallowed. "About what this means."

A flicker of something **darker** crossed his expression.

Then, **his phone rang.**

The air **shifted** instantly.

Cassian didn't move at first, his gaze still locked onto mine. Then, finally, he exhaled and pulled the phone from his pocket.

His entire body **went rigid**.

Something **cold and dangerous** settled in his eyes.

I frowned. "What is it?"

Cassian didn't answer immediately. He turned, pressing the phone to his ear.

Then—his voice dropped into something I had never heard before.

Pure, murderous fury.

"You have five seconds to tell me why you're calling."

I stiffened.

The silence that followed was **thick**, tense, filled with something **deadly**.

Then, slowly, Cassian turned back to me.

And the look in his eyes—**possessive, protective, ruthless**—made my blood turn to ice.

"Pack a bag," he ordered.

I blinked. "What? Why?"

He ended the call, slipping the phone back into his pocket.

Then—his jaw clenched.

"Because someone just put a price on your head."

Cassian's POV

Someone was about to **die.**

I stormed through the penthouse, my mind already **spinning through every possibility, every enemy who would dare to take what's mine.**

Isla stood frozen, her arms wrapped around herself. **A storm of confusion and fear.**

I had **just claimed her.**

And now, the world wanted to **take her from me.**

I wouldn't let them.

"Cassian," she said, voice tight. "Who?"

I clenched my fists. "Viktor wasn't working alone."

Her breath caught. "But you—"

"I should have killed him slower." My voice was ice. **A promise of blood.**

Her lips parted, but before she could speak, I crossed the room in two strides and **cupped her face in my hands.**

She **shivered** beneath my touch.

"Listen to me." My voice was **low, dark, unshakable.** "You're not safe here."

She swallowed. "Where are we going?"

I brushed my thumb over her cheek, letting my grip **tighten slightly**, reminding her that she **wasn't going anywhere without me.**

"Somewhere no one can touch you."

Her lashes fluttered. "And if I say no?"

A slow, **wicked smirk** curled my lips.

"You won't."

She exhaled sharply, frustration flaring in her eyes. But she didn't **argue**.

Because deep down, she knew.

She was already mine.

And now?

Now, I was going to prove to the world that if anyone tried to take her...

I would burn everything to the ground.

CHAPTER TWENTY:
THE HUNT BEGINS

Isla's POV

A price on my head.

The words rang in my skull, **cold and unforgiving**, as Cassian's fingers tightened against my waist.

He was **calm**, too calm. **Like a man seconds away from snapping.**

My pulse hammered. "Who?"

Cassian didn't answer immediately. His gaze was **sharp, calculating**, as he pulled me closer, like he needed to feel my pulse to remind himself that I was still here.

Alive.

His voice was ice. **"Pack. Now."**

Something in his tone sent a **shiver down my spine**.

I swallowed hard. "Cassian, tell me—"

A gunshot split the air.

My breath **stalled.**

Cassian **moved instantly**, yanking me behind him as he reached for his own gun. **Two more shots.**

Too close.

I barely registered the sound of Cassian barking orders into his phone before he grabbed my wrist, **pulling me toward the elevator.**

"Cassian—"

"Not now," he snapped, his grip like **iron**, his body blocking mine as another shot **shattered the penthouse window.**

Whoever they were, they weren't waiting.

They were coming for me.

Panic **coiled in my chest.** "We can't just run—"

Cassian's **snarl** made my stomach flip.

"I don't run, Isla."

I swallowed hard. **No, he didn't.**

He hunted.

Cassian's POV

They had already made their first mistake.

They had come for **her**—in my home, on my territory.

And now, I was going to **bury them for it.**

The elevator doors slid open, revealing the underground parking garage. My car was already waiting—**engine running, reinforced, untraceable.**

Luca was standing beside it, gun drawn, his face set in a **grim mask.**

"They hit fast," he said as we approached. "Professional. Not street-level."

I already knew that.

This wasn't random. This wasn't Viktor's remaining men playing revenge.

This was planned.

Luca's eyes flicked to Isla. "She's the target."

A growl **rumbled deep in my chest**.

Of course, she was.

I glanced down at Isla—her breath was shaky, her hands clenched into fists, but **she didn't crumble.**

Even now, when she knew what it meant to be mine, when she knew **what kind of men wanted her dead**, she stood tall.

I cupped her face, forcing her to look at me. **"You're safe."**

She exhaled, eyes stormy. "Am I?"

I smirked. **"As long as you don't run from me again."**

A flash of something **fierce and defiant** crossed her expression, but she nodded.

That was enough.

For now.

I turned back to Luca. "We need to move."

Luca slid into the driver's seat, and I pulled Isla into the car with me. The doors **locked** automatically, reinforced steel separating us from the outside world.

As we pulled onto the street, Isla shifted beside me. "Where are we going?"

My fingers **tightened around the gun in my lap**.

"To hunt."

Unknown Location

He was watching.

74

Through the grainy footage of a security feed, the man studied **Cassian Morelli's car** as it disappeared into the city.

He leaned back in his chair, exhaling smoke from his cigar.

So. Cassian still thought he could win.

The man smirked, tapping his fingers against the desk.

Cassian Morelli had spent his life **untouchable**, playing god over this city.

But now?

Now, he had a weakness.

His **little pet.**

The man chuckled darkly. **Not for long.**

Because Isla Thornton?

She would be **his soon.**

CHAPTER TWENTY-ONE: STOLEN IN THE DARK

Isla's POV

The tension in the car was **thick, suffocating**, like the calm before a storm.

Cassian sat beside me, one hand gripping his gun, the other clenched against his thigh. **Controlled rage. Calculated fury.**

But beneath the deadly calm, I could feel it.

He was unraveling.

Because someone had dared to put a price on **me**.

Someone had tried to take **what belonged to him**.

And Cassian Morelli?

He didn't share.

I swallowed hard, my fingers tightening around the seatbelt. "Where are we going?"

Cassian's gaze flicked toward me, his **gray eyes unreadable**. "To find the bastard who put a target on you."

His voice was smooth, **lethal**, a promise of **blood and violence**.

Luca, driving in the front seat, spoke without looking back. "We traced the bounty through underground channels. It's high. Too high for low-level players. Someone wants her bad."

My stomach twisted. "Who?"

Luca hesitated. "Still working on that."

Cassian exhaled sharply, his jaw **ticking with restraint**. "Then work faster."

The way he said it sent a **shiver through me**.

Because I'd seen him angry before. I'd seen him **ruthless, possessive, obsessive.**

But this?

This was different.

This was **personal.**

The car **swerved suddenly**, sending my heart slamming into my ribs.

"Shit." Luca cursed, gripping the wheel as he veered into a side alley.

"What the hell—" Cassian started.

Then, before he could finish, **something exploded.**

A violent **BOOM** rocked the street behind us, flames lighting up the night.

I **screamed**, my body **slamming into Cassian's chest** as the impact rattled through the car.

"Ambush," Luca growled, yanking the wheel hard to the right.

The car **skidded**, tires screeching against the pavement. Cassian's **arms locked around me**, keeping me pressed against him.

His heartbeat was steady. His breath **calm.**

Because this was what he **lived for.**

He pulled his gun, his voice **low and cold**. "How many?"

Luca's eyes flicked to the mirror. "At least three cars. Armed."

Cassian exhaled slowly, a smirk playing at his lips. **"Pathetic."**

My **pulse pounded**, adrenaline roaring through my veins. "What do we do?"

Cassian glanced down at me, his smirk **dark and knowing**. "We play."

Then—**he opened the door.**

I gasped. "Cassian, no—"

Too late.

He was already **moving**, stepping out of the car **like a god of war**, gun raised, his presence **all-consuming**.

And the second he fired—

All hell broke loose.

Cassian's POV

They thought they could take her.

That they could **touch what was mine.**

I stepped into the chaos, my gun **steady**, my mind razor-sharp.

The first shot **hit home**, a clean kill. The second—**just as lethal**.

But they kept coming.

A car skidded to a stop in front of me. The door swung open, a masked man stepping out, gun raised.

78

I smirked. **Too slow.**

I fired.

He **dropped instantly.**

Then—**a scream.**

Not mine.

Not my men.

Isla.

My heart **stalled.**

I twisted just in time to see her **ripped from the car,**
a black-clad figure dragging her into an alley.

No.

A feral **roar** tore from my throat, something wild and
unchained.

I moved. Fast. Deadly.

Another shot—straight between the eyes of the man
holding her.

He collapsed.

Isla **staggered back,** gasping for air, her eyes wide
with shock.

And then—**another set of hands grabbed her.**

Another man.

My **vision turned red.**

He yanked her around the corner, disappearing into
the shadows.

I followed.

Gun raised. **Killing anyone in my path.**

But by the time I reached the alley—

She was gone.

They had taken her.

Unknown Location

Pain.

That was the first thing I felt when I woke up.

A dull, pounding **ache** in my skull, like I had been hit.

I blinked against the darkness, my vision **swimming**, my wrists aching where they were **tied together.**

No.

No, no, no.

Panic slammed into my ribs.

I tried to move. **Tried to fight.**

But I was **restrained, trapped, stolen.**

Again.

A shadow moved in front of me. A man.

I squinted, my pulse **hammering**. "Who—"

A **chuckle.**

Low. Dark. **Familiar.**

Then, a voice I **never wanted to hear again**.

"Hello again, little dove."

I **froze.**

No.

It couldn't be.

He was supposed to be **dead.**

I swallowed hard, my blood turning to **ice.** "Viktor."

He **smirked**, stepping into the dim light.

"Miss me?"

Cassian's POV

She was gone.

Taken. **Again.**

My breath was **ragged**, my knuckles bloody from the man I had just **beaten to death.**

Luca stood beside me, gun still smoking. "We'll find her."

My jaw **locked.**

Of course, we would.

Because Isla Thornton belonged to **me.**

And if Viktor thought he could take her from me?

He had just made the last mistake of his life.

CHAPTER TWENTY-TWO: THE MONSTER AWAKENS

Isla's POV

Viktor **should be dead.**

Cassian had beaten him, broken him, **left him bleeding out in the dirt**.

And yet—he stood before me, alive, breathing, **smiling** like he had already won.

My pulse pounded, my wrists straining against the ropes that **bound me to the chair**.

I swallowed hard. "How?"

Viktor smirked, stepping closer. **Too close.**

"Did you really think Morelli killed me?" His voice was **mocking**, filled with amusement. "Oh, sweetheart. He's good, but not good enough."

My stomach twisted. "What do you want?"

He leaned down, brushing a strand of hair from my face.

I **flinched.**

Viktor **laughed**.

"What I've always wanted." His voice dropped, low and cruel. "To take what belongs to Cassian."

Fury flared through me. "I don't belong to anyone."

His smirk widened. "Oh, you do. But now?" He tilted his head, eyes gleaming. "Now, you belong to me."

I **jerked against the ropes**, heart slamming. "Cassian will kill you."

Viktor exhaled a slow, deliberate breath. "Yes, he'll come for you. And when he does?" He grinned. "I'll be waiting."

A trap.

He had taken me to **lure Cassian in.**

To break him.

To **make him bleed.**

I clenched my jaw. "You think he'll just walk into your hands?"

Viktor chuckled. "Oh, he won't walk." His blue eyes gleamed. **"He'll run."**

A sick feeling curled in my stomach.

Because I knew **he was right.**

Cassian wasn't coming for me **carefully, strategically.**

He was coming like a **fucking storm.**

And when he found Viktor?

There would be nothing left.

Cassian's POV

I was **going to kill him.**

No hesitation. No mercy. **No fucking survivors.**

Luca gripped his gun, his expression tense as he matched my stride. "We have a location."

I didn't slow. "Where?"

"A warehouse on the west side. Unmarked. Guarded."

My **jaw ticked**. "Not for long."

Luca exhaled. "You know it's a trap, right?"

I turned to him, my vision **tinted in red**. "I don't give a damn."

Luca cursed under his breath, but he didn't argue. **Because he knew.**

He knew that **no force in this world** could stop me from getting to Isla.

They had touched **what was mine.**

And now?

I was going to bury them for it.

Unknown Location – Isla's POV

Viktor leaned against the desk, **watching me**, waiting for me to break.

Waiting for **fear**.

But I wouldn't give it to him.

Not when I knew Cassian was coming.

Not when I knew **what kind of man he was.**

A predator. A monster. A man who **didn't lose.**

Viktor exhaled. "You're quieter than I expected."

I lifted my chin. **"I'm waiting."**

His smirk faltered. "For what?"

I **met his gaze**, my voice unwavering.

"For him."

Viktor's expression **darkened**, his body **tensing**.

Because he knew.

Cassian wasn't just coming.

He was **already here.**

Then—**gunfire.**

Viktor cursed, pushing off the desk as the sound of **men screaming** echoed from outside the room.

My breath **hitched.**

He was **here.**

Cassian Morelli had found me.

And now?

Hell was about to rain down.

Cassian's POV

I **moved fast.**

Gunfire cracked through the air, but it barely registered.

They were nothing.

Nothing but obstacles between me and **her.**

My breath was steady. My grip on my gun was firm. My heartbeat was **a war drum in my chest.**

One by one, I took them down.

Bullets. Blades. Blood.

They didn't deserve quick deaths.

They deserved to **know**.

They deserved to see **the devil in my eyes before I ended them.**

I reached the final door.

The one standing between me and **Isla.**

A slow, deep inhale.

Then—I kicked it open.

Viktor spun, **gun raised.**

Isla's **eyes met mine.**

Relief. Shock. **Something else.**

And Viktor?

He smirked.

"I was wondering when you'd get here."

My **finger tightened on the trigger.**

No more words.

No more **games.**

I was going to **end this.**

Because Isla was **mine.**

And I'd tear the world apart to keep her.

CHAPTER TWENTY-THREE: VENGEANCE IS MINE

Cassian's POV

I had never been a patient man.

And Viktor had just **run out of time.**

The moment I stepped into the room, my gun locked on him, **his smirk faltered.**

Good.

I wanted him to **know.**

To see his **death written in my eyes** before I made it real.

He lifted his gun, but **I was faster.**

A single shot.

Straight to his **shoulder.**

He **staggered back**, cursing, his gun clattering to the floor.

Not dead.

Not yet.

Behind him, **Isla gasped**, her body **tensed in the chair,** her wrists **red from the restraints.**

Mine.

They had tied her up. **Tried to break her.**

I saw **red.**

Viktor clutched his bleeding shoulder, **grinning through the pain**. "Took you long enough, Morelli."

I stepped closer, gun still raised. **Calm. Lethal.**

"No," I said smoothly. "I wanted you to wait."

Viktor's grin twitched. "And now what? You kill me?"

I smirked. **"Eventually."**

His eyes flickered, just for a second, with something **dangerous**. "You don't think this ends with me, do you?"

I tilted my head. "The difference between us, Viktor?" My grip **tightened on the trigger**. "Is that when I kill someone…"

I fired again.

This time, in his leg.

He **screamed**, falling to one knee.

"…they stay dead."

Viktor's breaths came in **ragged gasps**, his body trembling as **blood pooled beneath him**.

Good.

I wanted him to feel it.

To feel every ounce of pain, every **second of suffering** before I ended him.

Because he had taken **what was mine**.

And no one touched **what belonged to me** without consequence.

I turned slightly, my gaze locking onto **Isla**.

Her eyes were wide, **stormy with something unreadable**.

Not fear.

Not relief.

Something darker.

Something **dangerous.**

A war between **what she knew was right and what she could no longer deny.**

Viktor coughed, dragging my attention back. "You can kill me, Morelli..." He let out a weak chuckle. "But that won't change what she is."

My jaw ticked. "And what's that?"

His bloody lips curled.

"The one thing you can never tame."

A slow, **primal rage** built inside me.

Because he was wrong.

Isla wasn't **something to be tamed.**

She was **something to be claimed.**

And I had already **won.**

I lifted my gun. "Goodbye, Viktor."

His smirk barely had time to fade before I **pulled the trigger.**

A clean shot.

Straight to the **heart.**

This time, **he didn't get back up.**

Isla's POV

I had never seen someone die before.

Not like that.

Not with such **cold precision.**

Cassian had shot him like it was **nothing.** Like Viktor was just another problem to be erased.

Because to Cassian? **That's all he was.**

I shuddered, my wrists still aching from the ropes.

Cassian turned to me, his gray eyes **unreadable** as he reached forward, **cutting my restraints loose.**

I inhaled sharply as my hands **fell into my lap,** my skin tingling from the rush of **freedom.**

But was I really **free?**

His fingers brushed against mine.

I stiffened.

He **noticed.**

His gaze flicked up to mine, his expression **calm but firm.** "Are you hurt?"

I swallowed. "No."

Silence.

Heavy. Suffocating.

I should have thanked him. Should have been **grateful**.

Instead, all I could feel was the crushing weight of **what I had just seen.**

Of what it **meant.**

Cassian had just killed for me.

**And I wasn't sure if I wanted to run from him…
or toward him.**

I stood on **shaking legs**, my breath unsteady. "This…
this isn't normal."

Cassian's smirk was slow, **wicked**. "What part?"

I exhaled sharply. "All of it."

His hand lifted, **trailing a slow path up my arm**,
forcing me to **feel every inch of his claim.**

"This is your life now, Isla." His voice was **smooth,
possessive.** "You can pretend all you want."

His fingers tilted my chin up, forcing my gaze to lock
onto his.

"But we both know you don't want to run anymore."

A shudder **ripped through me.**

Because he was **right.**

I hated him.

I **needed** him.

And the worst part?

I didn't **know the difference anymore.**

Cassian's POV

She was trembling.

Not with **fear.**

With **realization.**

She wasn't **free**.

Because she had **never wanted to be.**

I cupped her face, forcing her to **see it.**

To **feel it.**

To know—without a doubt—**who she belonged to.**

I leaned in, my lips brushing against her **ear**, my voice a deadly whisper.

"You're mine, Isla."

A shaky inhale.

A slow exhale.

Then—**she didn't pull away.**

She didn't fight me.

Didn't try to run.

She just **stood there, waiting.**

And in that moment, I knew.

She was **done pretending.**

CHAPTER TWENTY-FOUR: THE FINAL SURRENDER

Isla's POV

I should have run.

The moment Cassian **killed Viktor**, the second the blood **stained the floor**, I should have fought, screamed, clawed my way out of his grip.

But I didn't.

I just **stood there**, frozen in the space between **fear and desire**, between **hatred and something much darker**.

Cassian's hands still **framed my face**, his breath warm against my lips, his body **crowding mine, owning the air I breathed**.

I should run.

But I didn't want to.

Because deep down, I already knew the truth.

I had never wanted to **escape him.**

I had only wanted to **see if he would chase me.**

His **gray eyes burned** into mine, sharp with **triumph**, as if he could see the war raging inside me.

His grip **tightened**, his voice **low, final.**

"You're done fighting me."

I swallowed hard, my **pulse slamming** against my ribs.

He tilted my chin up, his thumb brushing over my lower lip. **Slow. Taunting.**

"Say it," he murmured.

My breath **shuddered**.

Because he wasn't asking.

He was **commanding**.

I **shouldn't**.

I **couldn't**.

But I did.

"…I'm done fighting you."

His **smirk deepened**, something dark and victorious gleaming in his eyes.

"Good girl."

A violent shiver ran through me.

Because the words didn't just **undo me**.

They **branded me**.

Cassian's POV

She had finally **broken**.

No more running. No more defiance. No more pretending she could ever be **anything but mine**.

I let my fingers **trail down her throat**, feeling the wild thrum of her pulse.

She was **shaking**.

Not with fear.

94

With **realization.**

With **submission.**

I leaned in, my lips **grazing her jaw**, my voice smooth as silk.

"You never really wanted to leave, did you?"

She sucked in a shaky breath.

I dragged my lips lower, just enough to feel the way her body **shuddered beneath my touch.**

"I…" She hesitated.

Waiting. Fighting. **Losing.**

Then—she whispered the words that sealed her fate.

"No."

My smirk was slow, wicked, **unforgiving.**

I grabbed her wrist, pressing her palm against my chest, forcing her to feel the **steady, unshakable rhythm of my heartbeat.**

"You feel that?" I murmured.

She nodded **slowly**, her breath uneven.

I exhaled, letting my forehead brush against hers.

"It beats for you, Isla."

A shaky **exhale.**

A pause.

Then—she finally broke.

She **collapsed against me**, her body molding into mine, her hands **clutching at my shirt like she was afraid to let go.**

I let her.

I let her **hold onto me, sink into me, become part of me**.

Because she already was.

Because now, she knew it too.

And now?

Now, there was **no escape.**

Not from me.

Not from us.

Not ever.

CHAPTER TWENTY-FIVE: NO WAY BACK

Isla's POV

The moment I **collapsed against him**, I knew.

There was **no escape**.

Not from Cassian. Not from the **dark, unrelenting gravity** that pulled me toward him.

Not from **this.**

I had fought him. **Fought this.**

And I had **lost.**

I felt the **slow rise and fall of his chest**, the way his fingers **curled around my waist**, pressing me closer, as if he could **feel me slipping and refused to let me go.**

A shudder ran through me.

Because I didn't **want** him to let me go.

His breath was **warm against my temple**, his grip **firm, possessive, absolute.**

"You finally understand, don't you?"

His voice was smooth, **dangerous**, a whisper wrapped in steel.

I squeezed my eyes shut, my fingers **digging into his shirt.**

Yes.

But I couldn't say it.

Not yet.

Not when the last fragile part of me still **clung to the illusion of control.**

Cassian exhaled slowly, his **lips grazing my jaw**, his voice a dark **promise.**

"There's no way back, Isla."

My stomach **tightened.**

I knew.

I knew the second I **chose him**, there would be no **undoing it.**

No escaping.

No pretending I could ever be **anything but his.**

I **tensed** as he lifted my chin, forcing me to meet his gaze.

His **gray eyes burned**, sharp with **triumph and something deeper—something I wasn't ready to name.**

"Say it," he murmured.

A **command.**

I swallowed hard. "Say what?"

His lips curled into a slow, **wicked smirk.**

"That you're mine."

A violent **shiver** tore through me.

Because I had already **lost.**

I had already **given in.**

And I wanted him to **know it.**

I parted my lips, my **breath shaking.**

"…I'm yours."

Cassian's smirk **faded**—replaced by something **deadlier, more dangerous.**

Satisfaction. **Possession.**

A **vow sealed in fire.**

Then—his **lips crashed into mine.**

And just like that, the last of my resistance **shattered.**

Cassian's POV

She was **mine.**

Finally. **Completely.**

And now?

Now, she would **never forget it.**

I deepened the kiss, my fingers tightening around her waist, **trapping her against me,** making sure she felt **every inch of the power I had over her.**

Her breath hitched, her body **melting into mine,** her hands **gripping my shoulders as if she needed something to hold onto.**

I smirked against her lips.

Because I was **all she had left.**

I pulled back slightly, just enough to see the **storm in her eyes,** the way her lips were **slightly parted,** her breath **ragged, unsteady.**

She was still **processing what she had just done.**

What she had just **given me.**

I traced a slow, deliberate path down her spine, feeling the **shudder that tore through her.**

"You're done running," I murmured.

A slow, **desperate inhale.**

Then—she nodded.

That was **all I needed.**

I grabbed the back of her neck, tilting her head up, **forcing her to see the truth.**

The truth that **she was mine.**

That she had **always been mine.**

That now?

There was no way back. For either of us.

CHAPTER TWENTY-SIX: WHAT IT MEANS TO BE HIS

Isla's POV

The second I **gave in**, I felt it.

The shift. The **finality**.

Like a door had closed behind me, **sealing me in**, leaving no way back.

Cassian's hands were still **firm on my body**, his lips **still warm against mine**, his presence **all-consuming**.

I had lost.

I had surrendered.

But now—**I had to live with that choice.**

I pulled back slightly, trying to steady my breath, trying to regain **some sense of control**.

Cassian's **gray eyes burned into mine**, his smirk slow, dangerous. **Triumphant.**

"Now you understand," he murmured.

A slow, **shuddering exhale** escaped me.

Because I did.

I **understood everything.**

That there was no escape.

That I had never really **wanted one.**

That I was **his now, and he had no intention of ever letting me go.**

I swallowed hard, my pulse **still racing.** "What happens now?"

Cassian's fingers **trailed along my jaw,** slow, deliberate. "Now?"

His smirk deepened. **"Now, you learn what it means to be mine."**

A sharp **shiver** ran through me.

Because I knew, in that moment, **I had given him everything.**

And he had no intention of **ever giving me back.**

Cassian's POV

She still looked like she wanted to **run.**

Not because she didn't want me.

But because she **did.**

Because she had just given up the one thing she had fought for so long—**control.**

I tilted her chin up, my fingers **tightening ever so slightly,** forcing her to look at me.

She had always been beautiful.

But now?

Now, she was **mine.**

Her breath was uneven, her pulse **wild beneath my touch,** her lips **still parted from my kiss.**

She was **ruined.**

And I had been the one to **ruin her.**

102

I leaned in, my lips grazing her ear. **"Do you regret it?"**

Her breath **hitched**.

She knew what I was asking.

Not just about tonight.

About **everything.**

About **belonging to me.**

Her fingers **tightened against my shirt,** like she was holding onto something unseen.

Then—she whispered the truth.

"…No."

A slow, wicked smirk curled my lips.

Victory.

Because **now,** she knew it too.

There was **no way back.**

Not for her.

Not for me.

Not for **us.**

CHAPTER TWENTY-SEVEN: NO MORE DOUBT

Isla's POV

I couldn't breathe.

Not because I was afraid.

But because the **truth was finally settling in.**

Cassian Morelli had won.

And now? Now, I had to live with what that meant.

His hands were still on me—**firm, steady, claiming.** His fingers **trailed down my arm**, burning into my skin with every slow, deliberate touch.

"Say it again," he murmured.

A shiver ran down my spine. "Say what?"

His lips brushed against my jaw. **"That you're mine."**

My breath hitched.

Because he was still **pushing me.**

Still **testing me.**

Still making sure I knew—**there was no way back from this.**

I clenched my fists. "You already know."

Cassian chuckled, dark and low. **"I want to hear you say it."**

I exhaled shakily, my pulse hammering.

I had already given in.

Already **surrendered**.

So why did it feel so **impossible to say out loud?**

His fingers **tightened** around my waist. **"Say it, Isla."**

I swallowed hard. "I…"

His grip **tightened**. "Louder."

A violent **shudder** ran through me.

And then—finally, I broke.

"I'm yours."

Cassian **stilled.**

Then—his smirk was slow, dangerous, **possessive beyond reason.**

"That's my girl."

His lips **crashed into mine**, stealing my breath, my last lingering resistance, my **very soul.**

And just like that, I was **ruined.**

Forever.

Cassian's POV

She was finally mine.

Completely. **Irrevocably.**

And now?

Now, she would **never forget it.**

I deepened the kiss, **owning every inch of her**, making sure she knew—**this wasn't just desire.**

This was **possession.**

This was **forever.**

Her breath hitched, her hands **gripping onto me like I was the only thing keeping her standing.**

And maybe I was.

Maybe she had spent so long **fighting me**, she didn't realize that **she was made for this.**

Made for **me.**

I pulled back, watching her **gasp for air**, her pupils blown wide, her pulse **wild beneath my fingertips.**

"No more doubt," I murmured.

She swallowed hard.

Then—she nodded.

And that?

That was all I needed.

She was mine.

And now?

Now, she would **never doubt it again.**

Let's dive deeper.

CHAPTER TWENTY-EIGHT: THE WEIGHT OF FOREVER

Isla's POV

I had given in.

And now, **I had to live with it.**

Cassian's grip on me was **firm, steady, unshakable**—like he could feel my hesitation, like he **knew** a part of me still struggled to understand what I had just done.

What I had **chosen.**

What he had **always known was inevitable.**

His thumb brushed over my pulse, feeling the erratic rhythm beneath my skin. **Testing me.**

"You're thinking too much," he murmured.

I swallowed hard. **Of course, I was.**

Because **what now?**

What happened when I stopped running? When I **let go of the fight completely?**

Who did that make me?

His fingers tilted my chin up, forcing me to meet his gaze.

Gray. Dark. **All-consuming.**

"You're mine, Isla," he said smoothly. "Say it again."

A tremor ran through me.

I had already said the words.

I had already **given him everything.**

But now—now I was **beginning to understand what that meant.**

And the realization **terrified me.**

I exhaled shakily. "Cassian—"

His grip **tightened**, his smirk slow, knowing. **"Say it."**

A violent **shudder** ran through me.

Because he wasn't just **pushing me to say the words.**

He was making sure I **felt them.**

That I **knew them.**

That I understood, in every fiber of my being, **there was no turning back.**

I licked my lips, my pulse hammering.

"…I'm yours."

Cassian's eyes **darkened.**

His smirk vanished.

His grip on me **tightened, possessive, unrelenting**.

Then—his lips brushed my ear, his breath warm, his voice a dark whisper.

"Forever."

A sharp **shiver** ran through me.

Because that?

That wasn't just a word.

That was a **sentence.**

And I had just **sealed my fate.**

Cassian's POV

She was **mine.**

Completely. **Irrevocably.**

And now?

Now, she had **finally realized it.**

I dragged my thumb along her jaw, feeling the way her breath **shuddered beneath my touch.**

She was still **processing.**

Still trying to understand the depth of what she had **just given me.**

What she had **just become.**

I tilted her chin higher, my smirk slow, dangerous.

"You finally understand," I murmured.

Her lashes fluttered. "What?"

I exhaled, brushing my lips against her pulse, letting my grip **tighten.**

"That you belong to me."

A slow, shaky inhale.

Then—she nodded.

And that?

That was all I needed.

Because now?

Now, she wasn't just mine in **words.**

She was mine in **every way that mattered.**

And she would never forget it again.

Let's dive even further into the **intensity, control, and possession.**

CHAPTER TWENTY-NINE: NO WAY BACK

Isla's POV

The moment I said the words, I knew.

This wasn't a game anymore.

I wasn't just **Cassian Morelli's captive.**

I was **his.**

Fully. **Completely.**

And now?

Now, I had to **live with it.**

His hands were still on me—**firm, steady, possessive.** His thumb **brushed over my pulse**, feeling the wild rhythm beneath my skin.

He could **feel my hesitation.**

He **knew** I was still processing what I had just done.

What I had **just given him.**

Cassian tilted his head, his gray eyes locked onto mine. **"What are you thinking, Isla?"**

I swallowed hard, my breath **shaking.** "I—"

He leaned in, his lips grazing my ear. **"Tell me."**

I exhaled sharply, my chest tight.

What was I thinking?

That I had spent weeks **fighting him**, trying to convince myself that I could ever truly **escape him.**

That I had believed I could **hate him.**

That I had refused to admit the truth for so long.

And now?

Now, there was **no going back.**

I lifted my gaze, my lips parting, my body still trembling.

"I don't know who I am anymore."

Cassian's expression didn't change.

If anything, his grip **tightened.**

"Then let me tell you." His voice was **smooth, deadly, absolute.**

"You're mine, Isla."

I **shuddered.**

Because I knew it was true.

Because **I wanted it to be true.**

Cassian exhaled slowly, watching me with **that knowing smirk.**

"You'll learn to live with it."

My breath hitched. "And if I don't?"

His smirk **faded**, his fingers tilting my chin up, forcing me to look at him.

"You already have."

A violent **shiver** ran through me.

Because he was **right.**

I had already **become his.**

I had already **fallen.**

And now?

Now, I wasn't sure if I ever **wanted to get back up.**

Cassian's POV

She was breaking.

Not in fear.

Not in weakness.

But in **acceptance.**

I had **pushed her, cornered her, claimed her.**

And now, she was finally **seeing it.**

I tilted her chin up, letting my thumb trace her **soft, parted lips.**

"You still think you have a choice?" I murmured.

Her breath was **shaky, uneven.** "I—"

I let my lips graze her jaw. "There's no more running, Isla."

A slow, **shuddering inhale.**

I smirked. "No more doubt."

Her fingers **curled into my shirt,** her pulse **wild beneath my hands.**

Because she knew.

She **knew.**

And now?

Now, I was going to make sure she never **forgot it again.**

CHAPTER THIRTY: OWNED IN EVERY WAY

Isla's POV

I had spoken the words.

I had **given in.**

But the weight of it **settled over me like a chain I had willingly placed around my own throat.**

I was **his now.**

Not just in words, not just in fleeting moments of surrender.

In every way.

And Cassian?

He would make sure I **never forgot it.**

His fingers **brushed my jaw,** slow, deliberate, as if savoring the **final victory written in my eyes.**

"No more doubts," he murmured.

A slow, violent shudder ran through me.

Because I knew, deep in my bones—**there were none left.**

Cassian Morelli had **taken everything.**

And I had **let him.**

His smirk was **slow, dark, unrelenting.**

"Good girl," he murmured, his breath warm against my lips.

A sharp, **traitorous thrill** shot through me.

Because those words?

They didn't just **undo me.**

They **ruined me.**

And Cassian **knew it.**

His grip on my waist **tightened,** pulling me even closer, ensuring I felt **every inch of his dominance** over me.

"You don't get to doubt anymore," he murmured, his voice a **dark promise.**

I swallowed hard. "I know."

His **smirk deepened,** his fingers **brushing against my pulse, feeling it hammer beneath his touch.**

"That's my girl."

A violent **shiver ripped through me.**

Because I was.

I **was his.**

And now?

There was **no going back.**

Cassian's POV

She was **shaking.**

Not with fear.

With **acceptance.**

With **realization.**

She had finally **fallen.**

And now?

Now, I would make sure she **never questioned it again.**

I tilted her chin up, forcing her to **meet my gaze, to feel the weight of what she had just given me.**

"No more pretending," I murmured.

She inhaled sharply, her fingers **digging into my shirt**, as if trying to hold onto something solid.

As if she knew—**I was all she had left.**

I smirked, my voice **dark, triumphant.**

"You belong to me, Isla."

A slow, **shaky breath.**

Then—**she nodded.**

That was all I needed.

Because now?

Now, she wasn't just mine in **words.**

She was mine in **every way that mattered.**

And she would **never forget it again.**

CHAPTER THIRTY-ONE: THE REALITY OF BELONGING

Isla's POV

I had surrendered.

I had spoken the words.

But now, I was starting to realize—**Cassian wasn't done with me yet.**

This wasn't just about saying I belonged to him.

It was about **proving it.**

His grip on me was **unrelenting**, his presence **demanding**, as if he could **sense** the small, lingering doubts still hiding deep inside me.

His **gray eyes burned into mine**, sharp and calculating, like he was waiting.

Watching.

Testing.

And I knew—if I hesitated, if I so much as **flinched**, he would **see right through me.**

I clenched my fists, **steadying my breath**, refusing to let him know how much he still unraveled me.

His smirk was **slow, dark, triumphant.**

"You're still thinking too much."

I swallowed hard. "I—"

Cassian **tilted my chin up**, his fingers firm, possessive.

"No more thinking." His voice was **silk-wrapped steel**. "No more questioning."

I let out a slow, **shaky breath**.

Because I knew what he wanted.

Not just my words.

Not just my surrender.

He wanted **all of me**.

Completely. **Irrevocably.**

I inhaled sharply. "Cassian—"

His smirk deepened, his grip **tightening just enough to remind me who was in control**.

"You already chose me, Isla," he murmured.

A violent **shiver** ran through me.

I had.

I had chosen him.

And now?

Now, I had to **face what that meant.**

Cassian's POV

She was still hesitating.

Still **processing**.

Still clinging to the last threads of **control she no longer had**.

I watched the war in her eyes, the **storm of emotions** she refused to say out loud.

And I decided—I wasn't going to wait for her to come to terms with it.

I was going to **make her.**

I brushed my thumb over her lower lip, my smirk slow, **dangerous**.

"Say it again," I murmured.

She **tensed**, her pulse hammering against my touch.

A slow, sharp inhale.

Then—**she whispered the words.**

"…I'm yours."

A dark, satisfied **growl** rumbled in my chest.

Because this time?

She didn't hesitate.

She didn't **flinch.**

She **knew.**

And now?

Now, she would **never doubt it again.**

CHAPTER THIRTY-TWO: THE WEIGHT OF HIS CLAIM

Isla's POV

I had spoken the words.

I had **given in**.

And now, I had to **live with the weight of what that meant.**

Cassian's grip on me was **firm, unyielding**, his **gray eyes dark with possession** as he studied me. **Reading me. Testing me.**

Because to him, **words weren't enough.**

He didn't just want my surrender.

He wanted my **absolute obedience.**

No hesitation. No resistance.

Only **acceptance.**

I swallowed hard, my pulse hammering against my ribs.

His fingers **trailed down my arm**, slow, deliberate. **Too soft for the storm brewing in his expression.**

"You still don't get it, do you?" he murmured.

A shiver ran through me. "Get what?"

Cassian's smirk was **slow, devastating. Predatory.**

"That there's no way back."

A slow, sharp inhale.

I already knew. **God, I already knew.**

But hearing him say it? **Feeling the certainty in his voice?**

It **wrecked me.**

"I… I know," I whispered.

His smirk **deepened.**

"No," he said smoothly. **"You think you do."**

His fingers **tightened,** his grip **possessive, demanding.**

"But I'm going to make sure you never forget it again."

A violent **shudder** ran through me.

Because I knew—**I wasn't ready for what that meant.**

Cassian's POV

She was still **processing.**

Still trying to **convince herself she understood.**

But she didn't.

Not yet.

Not fully.

I let my fingers drift along her jaw, tilting her chin **just enough to force her eyes to stay locked on mine.**

She still looked like she wanted to **run.**

Not because she didn't want me.

But because she **did.**

Because she knew—**the second she let go completely, the second she stopped thinking and just accepted that she was mine…**

She would **never escape me.**

And that terrified her.

Good.

I brushed my lips against her ear, my voice smooth, **absolute.**

"No more hesitation."

A slow, **shaky breath.**

She **exhaled,** her fingers **trembling** where they gripped my shirt.

Then—**finally, she nodded.**

My smirk **deepened.**

"Good girl."

Her breath **hitched,** her pulse hammering.

Because she knew—**this wasn't just about words anymore.**

This was about **proving it.**

And now?

Now, she **belonged to me.**

Completely.

Irrevocably.

Forever.

CHAPTER THIRTY-THREE:
THE LAST BETRAYAL

Isla's POV

I had surrendered.

I had given in.

But **I hadn't been ready for what came next.**

Cassian's grip was **still firm on me**, his **gray eyes dark and certain**, as if daring me to **doubt him again.**

I couldn't.

Because I **knew** now—there was no escaping him.

I had made my choice.

And yet, as I stood in his penthouse, **wrapped in the storm of his world,** I felt it.

The shift.

The **calm before a war.**

Something was coming.

Something **bigger, darker, inevitable.**

I could **feel it** in the way Cassian was **tense beneath his control**, in the way Luca and his men moved with **sharper urgency.**

Something was **wrong.**

I turned to Cassian, my stomach twisting. "What is it?"

His **jaw ticked**, his gaze flickering with **something unreadable**.

But before he could speak—

The glass windows shattered.

Cassian's POV

I moved before the first bullet hit.

Gun drawn. Isla behind me.

Luca was already **returning fire**, taking down the first set of intruders as **chaos exploded inside the penthouse**.

An ambush.

A declaration of war.

I could hear **shouting over earpieces**, my men moving to intercept, but I didn't give a damn about the fight.

I only cared about **one thing**.

Isla.

I turned, grabbing her wrist, **dragging her behind me as I moved toward the underground exit.**

But the second we reached the hallway—**the doors blew open.**

More men. **Armed. Waiting.**

I barely had time to react before a familiar voice cut through the gunfire.

A voice that made my **blood run cold**.

"Well, well, Morelli."

I stiffened.

No.

I turned, my gun still raised, and came face to face with **the one man I never expected to see again.**

Matteo Ricci.

My father's **old enemy.**

A man I had **buried years ago.**

And yet, there he stood, smirking, gun in hand, his men **outnumbering mine.**

Behind me, Isla **stilled.**

Matteo's gaze flicked to her, his smirk widening.

And then, **he said the one thing that made the world tilt beneath my feet.**

"You really didn't know, did you?"

I didn't speak.

Didn't **breathe.**

Because I could already feel it.

A secret I never saw coming.

Matteo exhaled a slow, satisfied sigh.

"She's not just a girl, Morelli."

He tilted his head toward Isla, his smirk sharp.

"She's a Ricci."

CHAPTER THIRTY-FOUR: THE WAR FOR HER

Isla's POV

Ricci.

The name echoed through my mind, slicing through me like a knife.

I **shook my head**, heart slamming into my ribs.

No.

No, this wasn't possible.

I wasn't—**I couldn't be—**

Cassian's fingers **tightened around my wrist**, grounding me, but when I turned to face him, his expression was something I had never seen before.

Rage. Possessiveness. A flicker of something darker.

As if, for the first time since I had met him, he wasn't sure what the **hell I was to him anymore.**

"You're lying," Cassian said, his voice low, **lethal.**

Matteo smirked. "Am I?"

He took a slow step forward, gun still in his grip, **but his attention was locked onto me.**

"Sweetheart," Matteo drawled, **mocking, cruel.** "Didn't your dear father ever tell you?"

I clenched my fists. "Tell me what?"

He exhaled a sharp, amused breath. "That you were never meant for Morelli."

A slow, sickening feeling coiled in my stomach.

Matteo's smirk deepened. "You were meant to be a Ricci."

I **staggered back.**

Because I already **knew** what that meant.

Blood. Power. **Marriage alliances in the underworld.**

I wasn't just **Cassian's by accident.**

I had been **promised to another.**

Cassian's POV

I barely heard Matteo's words over the roar in my ears.

Because Isla?

Mine.

She had always been mine.

And now—**some dead man walking was trying to rewrite fate?**

I lifted my gun. "You really think you can take her from me?"

Matteo **laughed,** shaking his head. "I don't have to take her, Morelli. She was never yours to begin with."

My **vision went red.**

But before I could pull the trigger—

Isla moved.

She **shoved me aside,** her voice sharp, **desperate.**

"Cassian, wait."

The betrayal sliced through me.

I turned to her, my jaw **ticking**, my breath **ragged**.

Her hands trembled, her lips parted, her **entire world crumbling around her.**

But she still **looked at me.**

And I knew.

She wasn't going anywhere.

Matteo clicked his tongue. "Come on, sweetheart. Let's not make this messy."

Isla's breath hitched, her fingers clenching at my shirt.

A slow, **deadly smile** curled my lips.

She wasn't moving.

She wasn't choosing them.

Because she had already **chosen me.**

I exhaled, cocking the gun in my hand.

"No, Matteo."

I smirked, stepping forward, **blocking Isla from his view.**

"This won't be messy."

I pulled the trigger.

And just like that—**the war ended.**

Isla's POV

Matteo hit the ground before he had the chance to react.

Blood **splattered across the floor,** the gun **clattering from his hand.**

Dead.

Gone.

My breath came in sharp, **ragged gasps.**

Cassian stood before me, his **gun still raised,** his body **calm, unshaken.**

Because this had never been a choice.

Not for him.

Not for me.

Cassian turned, his **gray eyes locking onto mine, unreadable, dangerous.**

I knew what he was asking.

Now, do you see?

My **fingers trembled.**

Because I did.

Cassian didn't just love me.

He didn't just **want me.**

He had **killed for me. Burned for me.**

And now, he was **waiting.**

Waiting for me to **do what I should have done all along.**

I swallowed hard, my pulse hammering.

Then—**I stepped closer.**

My fingers curled around **his wrist,** my breath still uneven, but my **decision made.**

Cassian exhaled slowly, smirking.

"Good girl."

And just like that, the war was over.

CHAPTER THIRTY-FIVE: THE LAST CHOICE

Isla's POV

The gunshot still echoed in my ears.

Matteo Ricci lay **lifeless at my feet**, the man who claimed I had never belonged to Cassian, the man who thought he could take me back.

But Cassian had **made his choice.**

Now, it was **my turn.**

The weight of his world pressed down on me, the **finality of it, the blood, the power, the darkness.**

I wasn't the same girl I had been when I first met him.

I had fought. I had **run.**

But now?

I wasn't sure I **wanted to anymore.**

Cassian turned to me, his **gray eyes sharp, waiting.**

He didn't speak.

Didn't demand.

Because for the first time, **he didn't have to.**

I already knew what he was saying.

What he was **asking.**

Now do you see?

I swallowed, my hands **shaking**, my pulse **thundering**.

I had two choices.

Step away. Leave.

Or **step forward.**

Into **his world. His claim. His darkness.**

The choice should have been easy.

But it wasn't.

Because when I looked at him, when I **felt the way he watched me**, waiting for me to either **run or stay**, I knew—

I was already his.

I had always been his.

And I always would be.

I let out a slow, shuddering breath.

Then—**I stepped forward.**

Cassian exhaled slowly, his smirk **dark, victorious**.

"You finally understand."

I did.

I **did.**

My fingers **curled around his wrist**, my breath still uneven, but my choice **made**.

Cassian tilted my chin up, his voice smooth, **dangerous**.

"No more doubts, Isla."

I swallowed hard.

And whispered the last words that sealed my fate.

"No more doubts."

Cassian's smirk deepened.

His hands **tightened on my waist**, his lips brushing against my ear, his voice a **dark promise.**

"Good girl."

And just like that, it was done.

I was **his.**

Forever.

EPILOGUE:
A KINGDOM BUILT ON BLOOD

Cassian's POV

Months later, the city still whispered her name.

They called her my queen.

They called her **the girl who chose the devil and never looked back.**

And they were right.

I watched from my office as Isla stood at the balcony, her gaze locked onto the city below—**our city.**

My smirk was slow, **satisfied.**

She had fought.

She had **run.**

But in the end, **she had come back.**

Because she knew, just as I did—

This was where she **belonged.**

Beside me.

With me.

Mine.

Forever.

The End

Made in the USA
Monee, IL
02 March 2025

13232520R00083